BL ST ADV

I NEED A LUNCH BOX

by Jeannette Caines   pictures by Pat Cummings

HARPER & ROW, PUBLISHERS

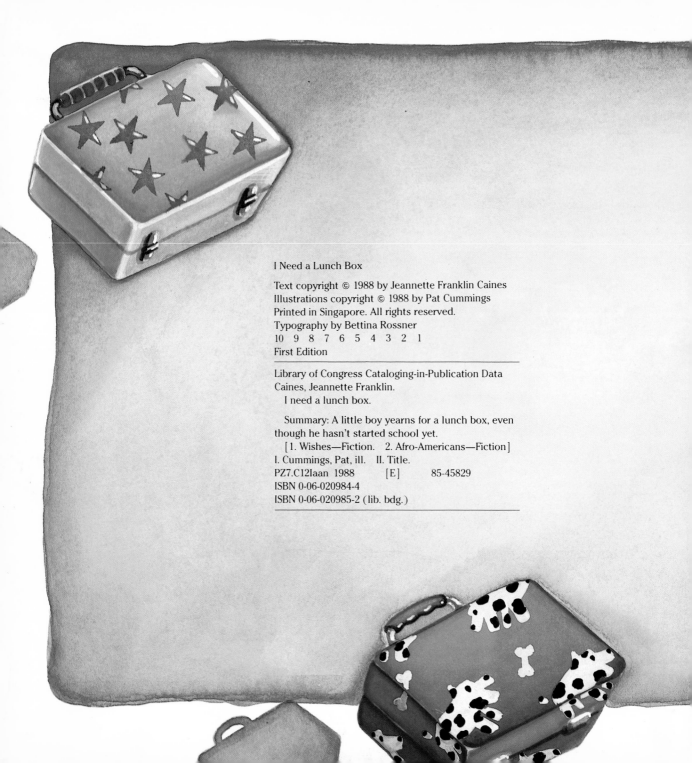

I Need a Lunch Box

Text copyright © 1988 by Jeannette Franklin Caines
Illustrations copyright © 1988 by Pat Cummings
Printed in Singapore. All rights reserved.
Typography by Bettina Rossner
10 9 8 7 6 5 4 3 2 1
First Edition

Library of Congress Cataloging-in-Publication Data
Caines, Jeannette Franklin.
  I need a lunch box.

  Summary: A little boy yearns for a lunch box, even
though he hasn't started school yet.
  [1. Wishes—Fiction.   2. Afro-Americans—Fiction]
I. Cummings, Pat, ill.   II. Title.
PZ7.C12Iaan 1988   [E]   85-45829
ISBN 0-06-020984-4
ISBN 0-06-020985-2 (lib. bdg.)

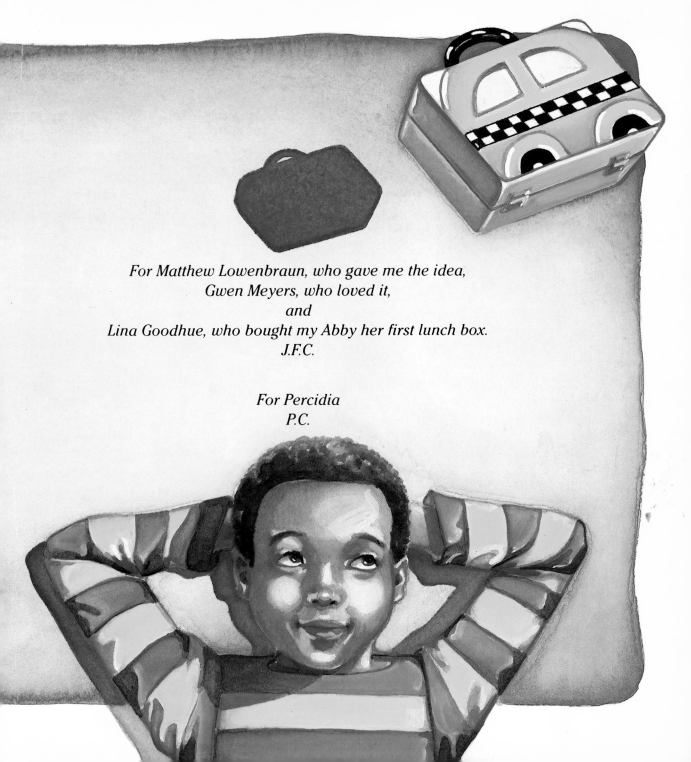

For Matthew Lowenbraun, who gave me the idea,
Gwen Meyers, who loved it,
and
Lina Goodhue, who bought my Abby her first lunch box.
J.F.C.

For Percidia
P.C.

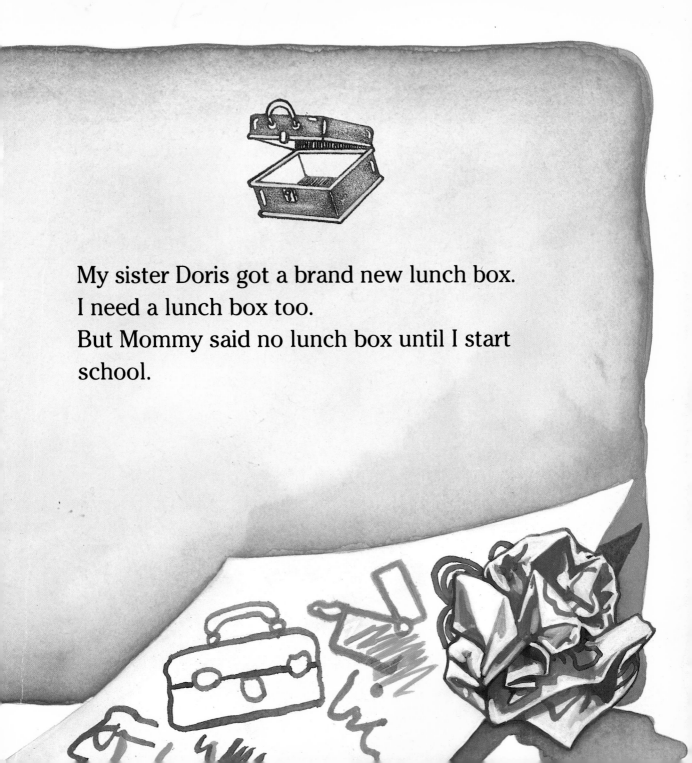

My sister Doris got a brand new lunch box.
I need a lunch box too.
But Mommy said no lunch box until I start school.

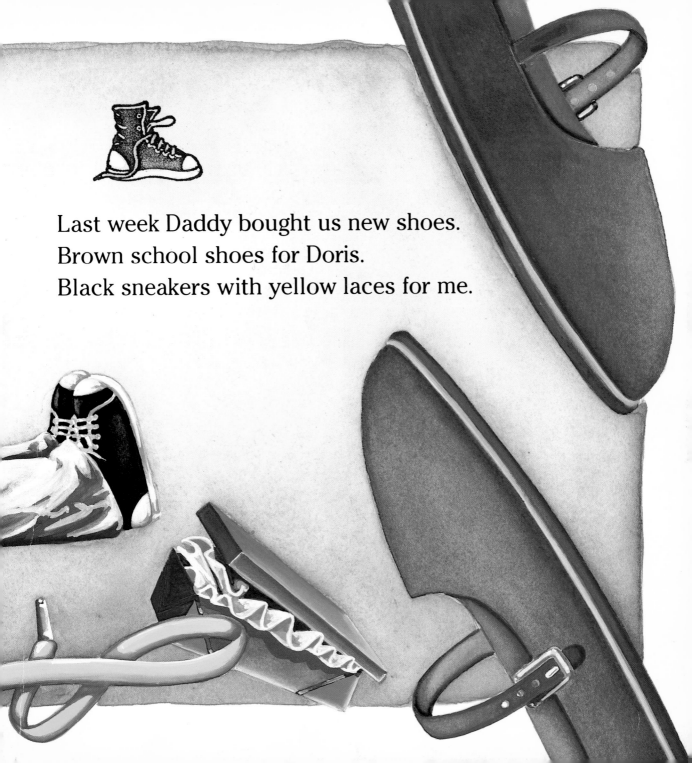

Last week Daddy bought us new shoes.
Brown school shoes for Doris.
Black sneakers with yellow laces for me.

We walked past the lunch box counter, twice.
I need a lunch box!

Doris got a pencil case with a ruler,
two new pencils, and two pink erasers.

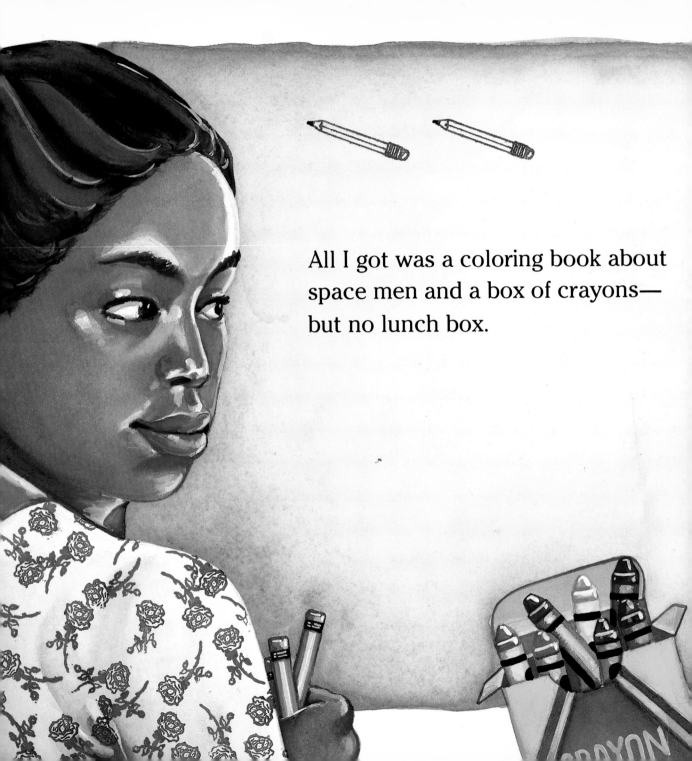

All I got was a coloring book about space men and a box of crayons— but no lunch box.

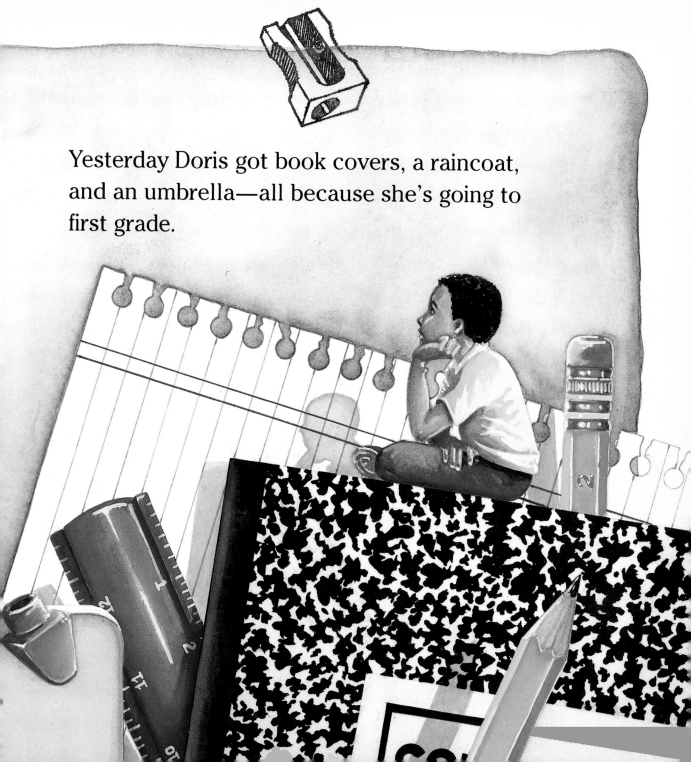

Yesterday Doris got book covers, a raincoat, and an umbrella—all because she's going to first grade.

If I had a lunch box I could keep
my crayons in it. Or my marbles,
or bug collection, or toy animals.

I dreamed I had five lunch boxes, one for every day.
Blue for Monday…

Green for Tuesday…

Red for Wednesday...

Purple for Thursday...

THURSDAY

Yellow for Friday.

I filled them with peanut butter and jelly
sandwiches, apples, oranges, chocolate cake,
cookies and pies and donuts.
And then we had a lunch box parade.

Doris starts school today.
I felt sorta bad when Mommy handed Doris
her brand new lunch box.
But then Daddy said, "I have a surprise for you.

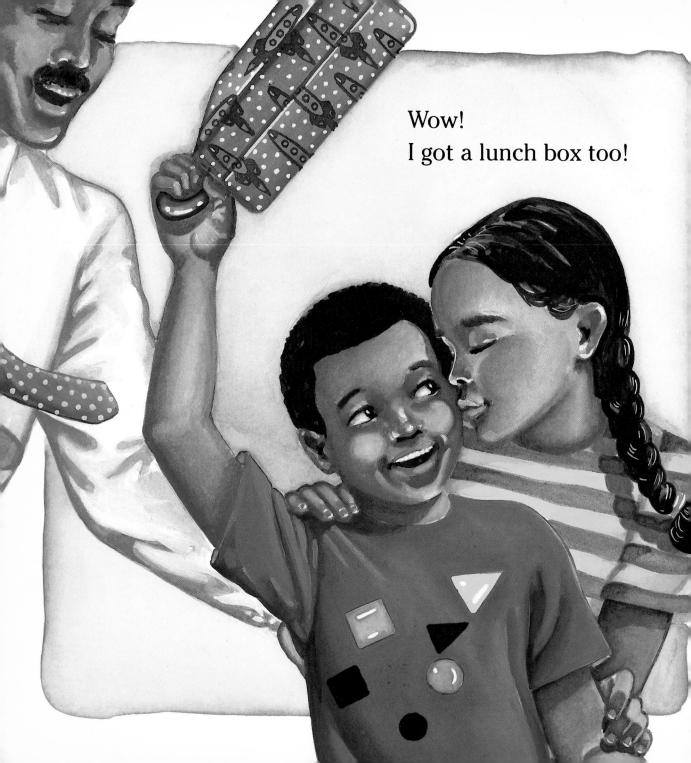

Wow!
I got a lunch box too!